WELLINGTON'S
BIG DAY OUT

STEVE SMALL

SIMON & SCHUSTER
London New York Sydney Toronto New Delhi

For Dad

SIMON & SCHUSTER

First published in Great Britain in 2022 by Simon & Schuster UK Ltd
1st Floor, 222 Gray's Inn Road, London WC1X 8HB

Text and illustrations copyright © 2022 Steve Small

The right of Steve Small to be identified as the author and illustrator of this work
has been asserted by him in accordance with the Copyright,
Designs and Patents Act, 1988

A CIP catalogue record for this book is available from
the British Library upon request

ISBN: 978-1-4711-9237-1 (HB)
ISBN: 978-1-4711-9239-5 (eBook)

Printed in China
1 3 5 7 9 10 8 6 4 2

One Saturday morning, Wellington woke up early. *Today is going to be a good day*, he thought.

All Saturdays were good, but this Saturday was *even* better. It was Wellington's birthday. He was a whole year older than he was yesterday . . .

I'm **definitely** *more grown up*, he thought.

He walked into the kitchen to see if his mum and dad would notice.

"Who is this gentleman?" said Mum. "What have you done with Wellington and why are you wearing his dressing gown?" said Dad.

"Why it IS Wellington!" they said together. **"Happy Birthday, Wellington!"**

Wellington was just enjoying his third pancake, when he noticed a present on the seat next to him.

He was very excited. But now that he was older, he gently picked it up and opened it carefully, the way his mum and dad would open their presents.

It was just what he wanted. A new jacket *exactly* like Dad's.

It was perfect.

Except that it was too big.

Seeing the look of disappointment on Wellington's face, Mum said, "Why don't you two go and visit the tailor in the city while I make a cake? Dad gets his jackets fixed there. You can see Grandad, too."

Wellington thought this sounded like a very grown-up thing to do and nodded happily.

When Wellington told the bus driver how old he was, the bus driver sighed. "I'm afraid that means you'll have to start paying for tickets now, Wellington." "Really?" Wellington said with a big smile.

Dad bought their tickets and they both took a seat.

"I've never seen anyone so happy about having to pay for something," his dad said, chuckling.

Wellington looked at the ticket. *It's only half fare, but it's a start*, he thought to himself.

The city was very busy and Wellington could hardly even see the sky through all the passers-by. He asked his dad for a shoulder ride.
"I thought everything looked big from the ground, but up here it's HUGE," Wellington said.

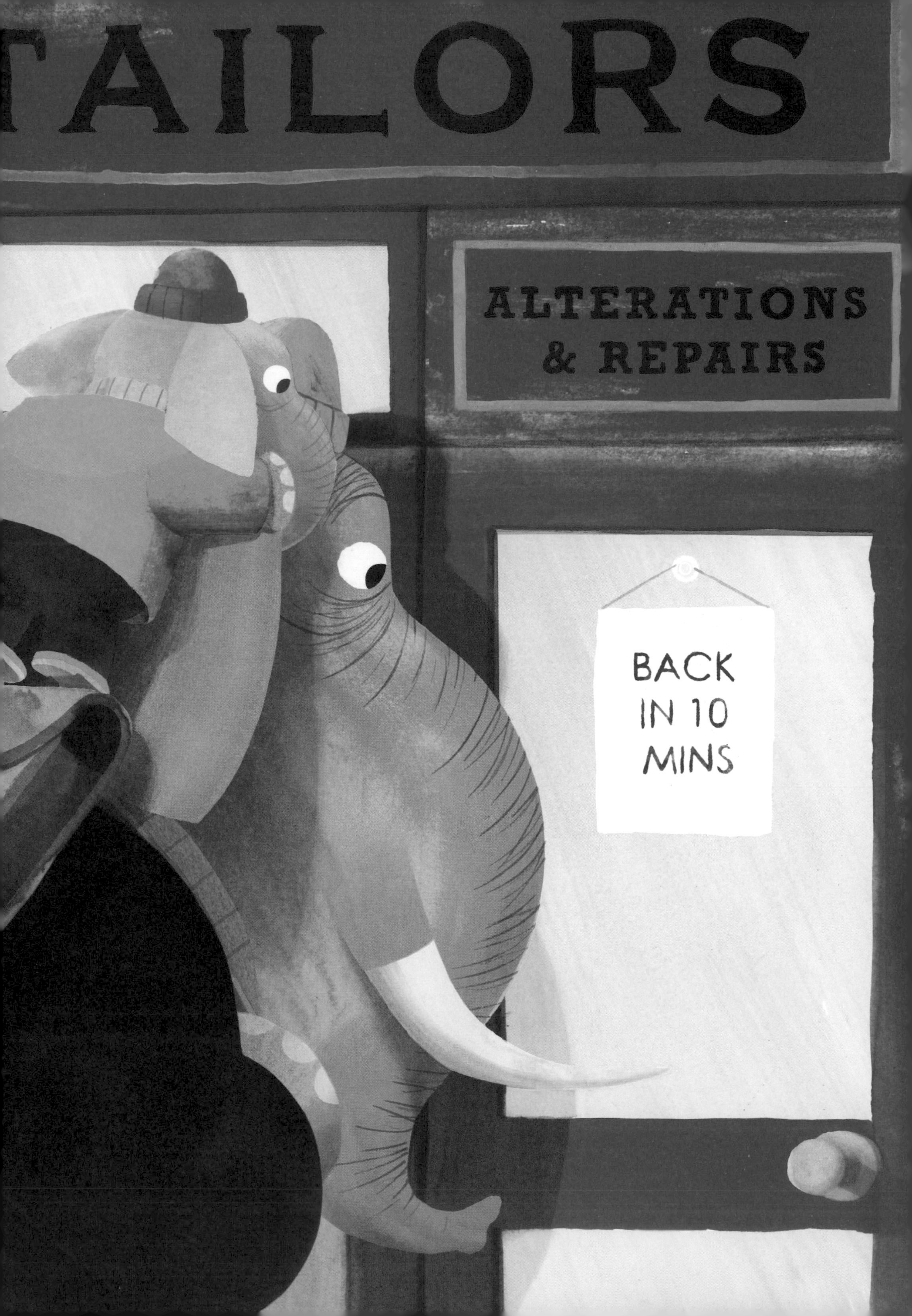
TAILORS
ALTERATIONS
& REPAIRS
BACK
IN 10
MINS

When they arrived at the tailor's, it was closed.
They decided to look around the music shop
next door while they waited for
it to open again.

Dad played a huge shiny tuba.

But when it was Wellington's turn,
and though he blew as hard as he could,
he could barely get it to make a sound . . .

Wellington's dad was about to ask if he wanted
to try something smaller, when he spotted the
tailor walking by.

P TAILORS

45

ALTERATIONS
& REPAIRS

BOB AND MARGE'S
MUSIC

47

GONE
TO
LUNCH

But when they got
outside, the tailor had gone.
This time they decided to wait
in the ice-cream parlour.

Dad chose the Super-Size Strawberry Sundae.

So did Wellington.

It was very, very good. But as tasty as it was,
Wellington couldn't quite finish it.

"It's just too **big**!" he gasped,
his tummy as tight as a drum.

Back outside, they found the tailor
had, once again, come and gone.

They both sighed.

Wellington's dad looked at his watch.
"It's time we went to Grandad's,"
he said, and they jumped in a cab.

HUFF PUFF
    HUFF PUFF
        HUFF PUFF

Grandad lived just outside the city.
The house was always fun to visit because
Grandad rarely threw anything away.
There was so much to see.

"Happy Birthday, Wellington!
My, how you've grown!" said Grandad.
Wellington smiled, but the smile didn't want to stay . . .

"Wellington's new jacket is too big," said Dad.

"It's not too big," said Wellington,
letting out a long sigh.

"I'm just

too

small."

Grandad sat beside him for a moment.
"I was just the same when I was young,
Wellington. All I wished for was to
grow up as fast as I could.

That's the trouble with wishes," he sighed.
"Sometimes they come true."

SIGH!

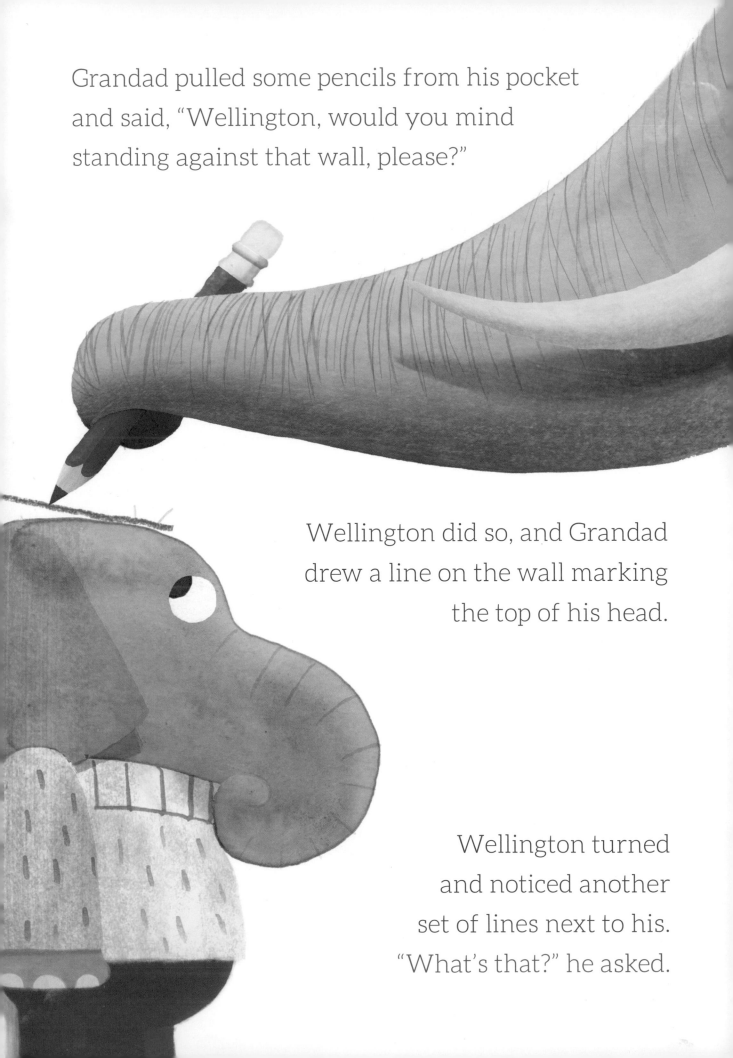

Grandad pulled some pencils from his pocket and said, "Wellington, would you mind standing against that wall, please?"

Wellington did so, and Grandad drew a line on the wall marking the top of his head.

Wellington turned and noticed another set of lines next to his. "What's that?" he asked.

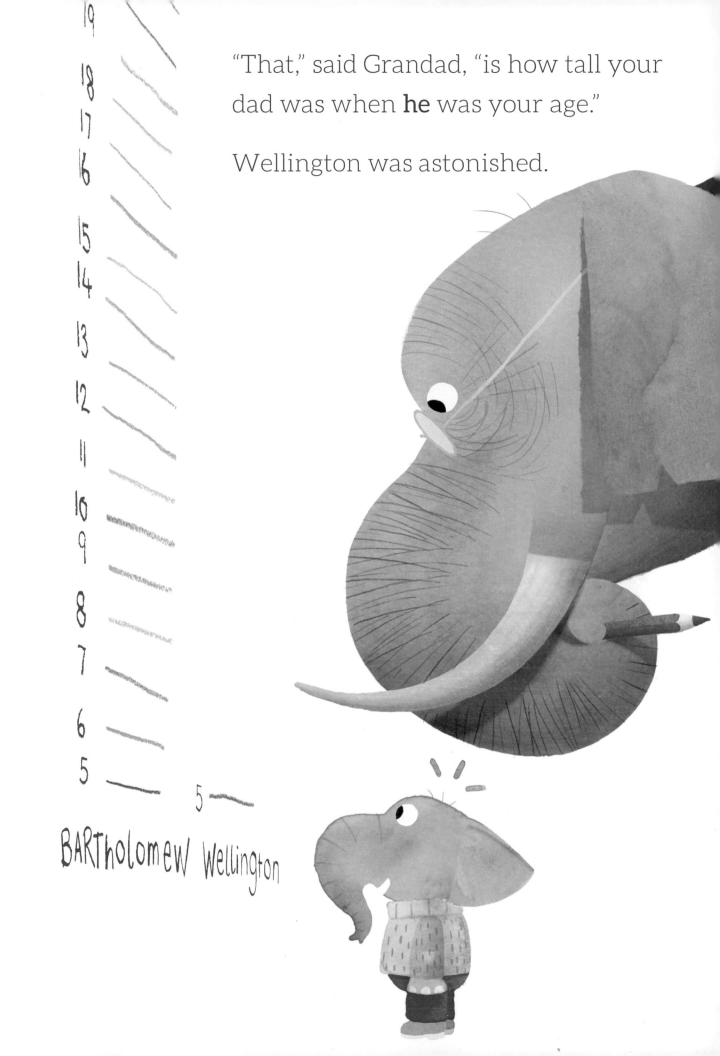

"That," said Grandad, "is how tall your dad was when **he** was your age."

Wellington was astonished.

19
18
17
16
15
14
13
12
11
10
9
8
7
6
5   5

BARTholomew Wellington

Grandad chuckled.
"Yes," he said, "your dad
was exactly the same height
as you are now."

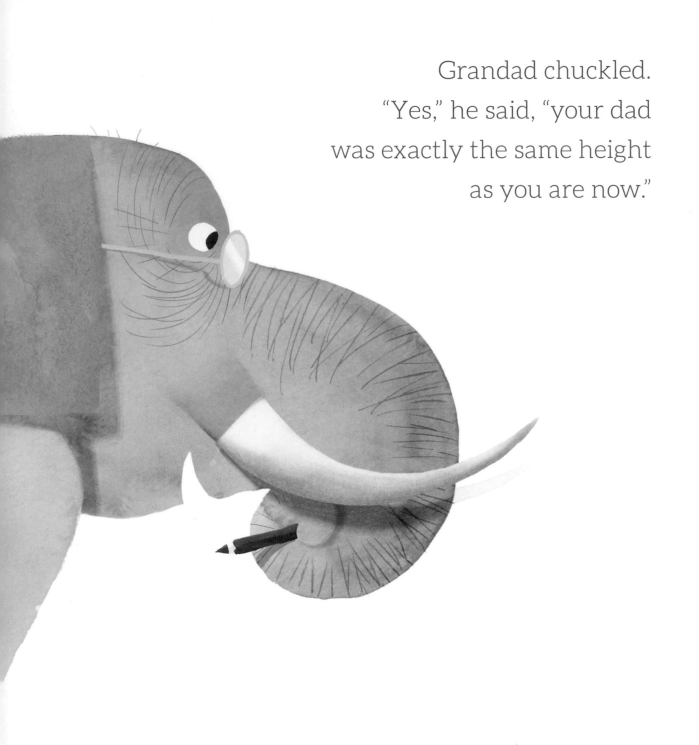

YAY   WOO
       WOO   YAY!

Wellington smiled
a very BIG smile.
And this time
it stayed there
for a while.

"Wellington?" said Grandad. "How would you like to go ice skating this afternoon?"

"What if they don't have skates that fit me?" Wellington asked.

"Why, that's easy," said Grandad. "I want you to have the ones I used to wear when I was your age."

"I think we'll miss the tailor if we go skating," said Dad.

Wellington thought about it for a moment.
He looked at the lines on the wall.

Then he looked at the jacket

. . . and at the skates.

"Maybe the jacket will fit me better
next year," he said.

They had a wonderful time at
the ice rink and stayed until
the sun went down.

And the skates?

They fitted perfectly.